SAME DIFFEREN

Black, Brown, Chocolate or Ivory;
White, Olive, Cream or Caramel;
It's still Skin by the way.

Curly, Coiled or Kinky;
Straight, Wavy or Crimpy;
It's real Hair any day.

Large, Deep or Roundly shaped;
Slanted, Tiny or Oval in shape;
With Gold, Hazel or dark hues;
They are true Eyes in all ways.

Eyes to see and eyes to stare,
Eyes to look and eyes to glare.
Be it Baby, Infant or Toddler,
Boy, Girl or Older,
They are all the same in every way.

ABOBAGUNWA

For Ethan and Isabella

Your courage, resilience and positive spirit inspired me to write this book.

For Craig

My biggest cheerleader and best friend.

To Every One

Regardless of our differences, I urge you to Stand Tall.

Written by TEJU AKANDE
Illustrated by Zeynep DURAL
Copyright © 2022 TEJU AKANDE

STAND TALL

WRITTEN BY **TEJU AKANDE**   ILLUSTRATED BY **ZEYNEP DURAL**

Buster lives in the village of Bon Mot with his mom, dad and little sister, Bean.

He loves playing video games and football with his friends. He supports Liverpool FC and his favourite player is Mo Salah.

Buster enjoys playing his violin.
He can often be found making
up tunes with his little sister.

One day, while he is playing football with his classmates, one of the boys, Jak, stops following the rules and ruins it for everyone. Buster asks Jak to follow the rules.

Jak shouts at Buster and calls him a horrid name. Buster feels sad. He bows his head and walks away.

Buster is quiet in the car on the way home. He stays in his room. He does not go outside to play football in the garden. He does not make up tunes on his violin with his sister.

At dinner time, Mom makes his favourite food in the world – Pizza. Buster takes just one bite and says he is not hungry. He goes back to his room.

Mom and Bean are worried.

When Dad comes home, Mom tells him that Buster has been very sad and quiet. He did not play football in the garden, he did not make up tunes with his sister and he did not eat his dinner.

Dad makes his famous chocolate brownies and they all go to Buster's room.

Buster is sitting on the floor playing with his lego.
He tells his family about the incident in the
playground and the horrid name that Jak called
him. He tells them how it hurt his feelings.

"I wish I looked the same as everyone else," Buster said sadly. A tear rolled down his cheek, "then no one will call me a horrid name like that."

Mom put her arm around Buster and said gently, "You and Jak may look different, but just like the birds that fly, it would be super boring if the only type of bird was the Pigeon."

"There would be no Robin, no Goldfinch and no Blackbird. We can say bye-bye to the Owl, the Red Kite and Peregrine Falcon."

"Our food comes from all around the world." said Mom.
" Hmm," said Buster, "I love sushi and jollof rice."

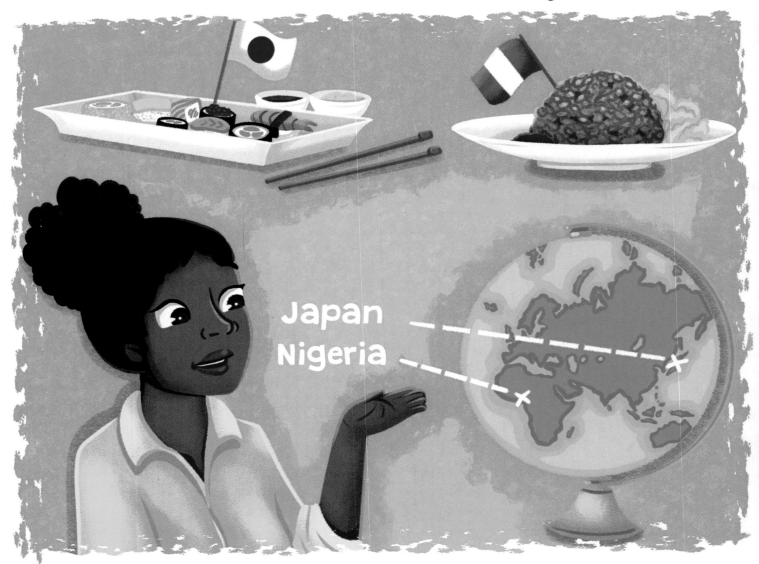

"Yes you do," smiled Mom. "Sushi is from Japan and jollof rice is from Nigeria. It would be very boring if all you ate was jacket potatoes!"

"Yuck!" Buster said, scrunching up his face.
"I love jacket potatoes!" shouted Bean.

"Imagine Liverpool without Mo Salah and F1 racing without Lewis Hamilton." said Dad. "Imagine Tennis without Serena Williams. Imagine there was no President Barack Obama."

"I love all those people." said Buster.
"Yes you do." said Dad. "And they all look like you."
Buster laughed. "Yes! They do look like me," he said.

"I am sorry you were hurt by the horrid name calling. Sometimes people say unkind things because they do not know better." said Mom.

"You are kind; you are fun..."

The next day, Dad takes Buster and Bean to School. Dad has a word with Mr Pettles, the Head Teacher.

Buster's friends run up to him. "Are you okay?" they yell. Buster is glad to see all his friends. He tells them about the birds and Mo Salah.

"Imagine Manchester United without Marcus Rashford, said Peter.
"Imagine Arsenal without Bukayo Saka," said Dan.

"Imagine Manchester City without Raheem Sterling," said Asher. "That would be terrible!" the boys exclaimed.

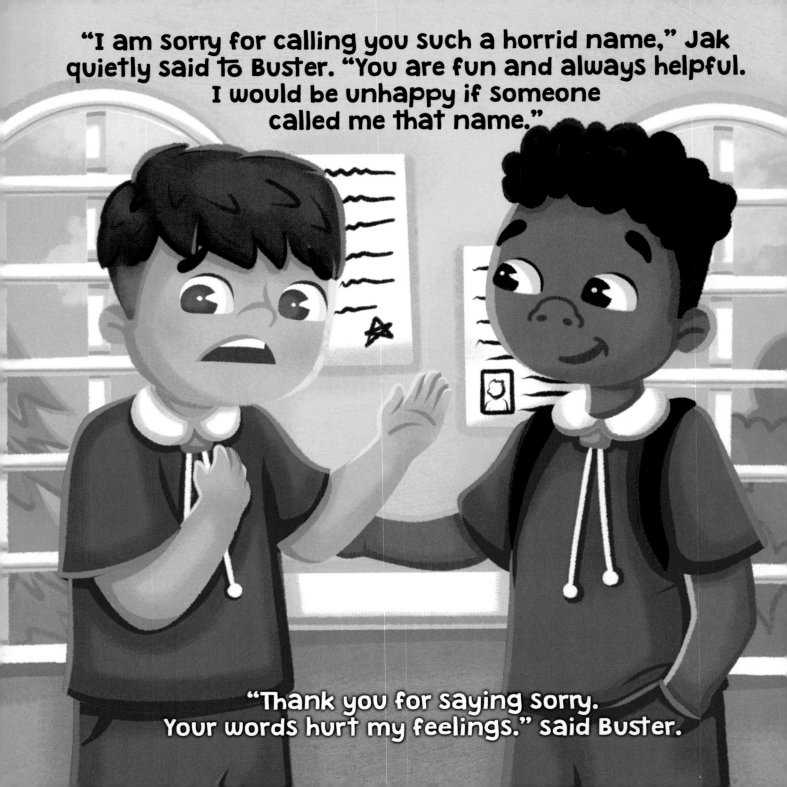

Buster, Jak and their friends play together.

"How was your day today?" Mom asks Buster.
"I had a great day!" said Buster. "I love school again!"

DAD'S FAMOUS BROWNIES

As a multiracial family, we realised the importance of having conversations about race, racial differences and racism with our children from a very young age. A great way we've found is to use food to have these difficult conversations.

Dad's Famous Brownies is one of our favourite family recipes. Many difficult topics have been discussed while making these yummy treats!

INGREDIENTS

- 150g (5 1/2oz) unsalted butter, plus extra for greasing
- 200g (7oz) dark chocolate
- 200g (7oz) light brown soft sugar
- 4 eggs, beaten
- 85 g (3 oz) plain flour
- 1 tbsp vanilla extract
- 1 tsp baking powder
- 2 tbsp cocoa powder, plus extra for dusting
- 1/8 tsp of salt
- 150g (51/2oz) white chocolate, roughly chopped
- 150g (5 + 1/2 oz) maraschino cocktail cherries, drained, chopped

DIRECTIONS

Preheat oven to 180C/350F/Gas 4.
Line a 9-inch square tin with baking paper and coat with nonstick spray. Set aside.

Melt dark chocolate and butter in a large mixing bowl.

Whisk sugar into the melted chocolate, then add eggs and vanilla extract. Mix well.

Add flour, baking powder, cocoa powder, chocolate chunks, cherries and salt.

Fold together until the flour is no longer visible. Do not over mix. Pour the mixture into the prepared pan and smooth over with a spatula or spoon.

Place in the oven and bake for 25-30 mins.

Remove from the oven, leave in the tin until cooled for about 1-2 hours.

Once cooled, lift them out of the tin onto a board.

Cut into squares. Sift over a little cocoa powder.

Store in an airtight tin.

Enjoy!

ABOUT THE AUTHOR

Teju lives in a little village in South England with her husband and 2 young children. They are a mixed British/Nigerian and Canadian family. She became inspired to start writing after her children experienced racial abuse and she could not find books that dealt with such a real world subject in an engaging and practical way. She aims to inspire and delight readers to feel confident, strong and proud about who they are.

If you enjoyed this book, we would appreciate it if you could take a minute to leave a review wherever you purchased the book. Your feedback encourages me to write more books. Best of all, it helps other adults discover this story so they can share it with the children in their lives. Don't forget to follow our Instagram account to be informed about future advetures of Buster and Bean!

[Instagram] @busterbeanchronicles

Made in the USA
Monee, IL
19 December 2023

50087332R00019